THE OLD PIG

THE OLD PIG

A WITTY AND TRADITIONAL VIEW

MARTIN WISCOMBE

Robinson Publishing Ltd
7 Kensington Church Court
London W8 4SP

First published in the UK by Robinson Publishing Ltd 1996

Special Edition for PAST TIMES, Oxford, England

A copy of the British Library Cataloguing in Publication data
is available from the British Library

ISBN 1-85487-272-9

Printed and bound in Hong Kong

10 9 8 7 6 5 4 3 2 1

For George and Jenny

UMBERLAND

THE CUMBERLAND, a lop-eared, coarse-boned pig, slow to mature like the Old English variety, finally died out in the 1960s, although it had become very scarce early in the century. It was almost always a white pig, but as always there were other regional varieties. This very fat, heavy-shouldered pig had been greatly valued for the excellence of its hams, bacon and sausages – many recipes for these popular products still bear the Cumberland name today.

'The sight of pigs with their noses in the trough does a man more good than any Methodist sermon.'

AUGUSTUS WHIFFLE

GLOUCESTER OLD SPOT

VERY POPULAR with the farmers and smallholders from the Vale of Berkeley, in Gloucestershire, these spotted pigs were kept in paddocks and orchards, and sometimes referred to as 'the Orchard Pig'. Officially known as Gloucestershire Old Spots, this pig has had a short history, the breed society first being formed in 1914. In recent times it has been fashionable to breed these pigs with just one or two spots and it should nowadays have lop ears.

'Man is more nearly like the pig than the pig would like to admit.'

ANON.

THE MIDDLE WHITE

THIS PIG has a very Oriental look about him and arose from the Yorkshire variety, along with the Large and Small Whites. Pigs of this type were first exhibited by Joseph Tuley, in 1852.

In the 1930s, three Middle Whites were exported to Japan, where more than 3,000 of their progeny were registered, and a memorial erected to them. The Emperor declared that he would never eat any other pork than the Middle White.

The breed enjoyed a long period of popularity up until the middle of the twentieth century, but is now quite rare.

The pig if I am not mistaken
Supplies us sausage, ham and bacon
Let others say his heart is big
I call it stupid of the pig.

OGDEN NASH

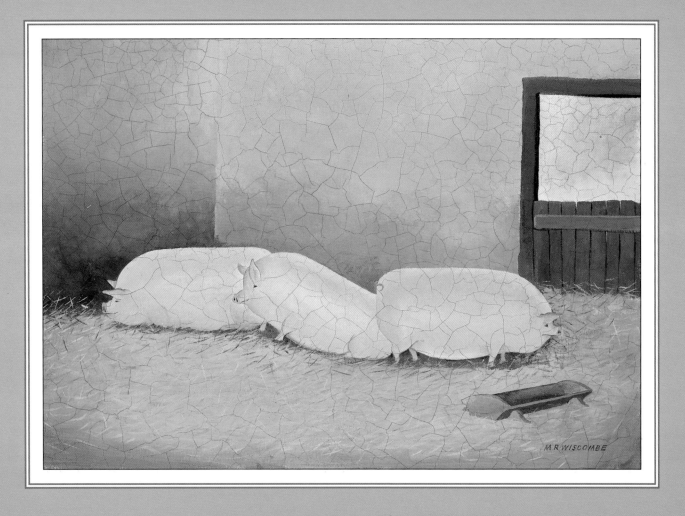

M.R.WISCOMBE

ORSET BLACK

BOTH THE Dorset Black and later the Improved Dorset, were bred by Frederick and John Coates, from Sturminster Newton in Dorset, in the nineteenth century. These small breeds were prone to become over-fat, and the Black Dorset was described as 'roly-poly', and was said to be so obese that it could scarcely walk – young pigs sometimes suffocated through overfeeding. When the taste for leaner pork began to make itself felt these breeds quickly died out.

To market, to market,
To buy a fat pig
Home again, home again,
Jiggety jig!

To market, to market,
To buy a fat hog,
Home again, home again,
Jiggety jog!

TRADITIONAL

M WISCOMBE

OLD CHESHIRE

ACKNOWLEDGED BY most authorities to be the largest pig breed, the Cheshire could weigh in at around 1,000 lbs when two years old, and in 1740 one was recorded at 1,605 lbs. They were originally bred in Cheshire, and belonged to the 'Old English' late-maturing type of animal, used almost exclusively for bacon production. The meat from such pigs would have had a very high fat content, 'fat bacon' being a much sought-after commodity in former times. The Old Cheshire was clearly declining in numbers by the end of the nineteenth century, and it is now sadly extinct.

Whose three hogs are these,
Whose three hogs are these?
They are John Cooke's, I know
*   them by their looks*

I found them in the pease
Go pound them, go pound them,
I dare not for my life,
No, for thou know'st John Cooke
*   very well,*
But better thou know'st his wife

TRADITIONAL

OLD YORKSHIRE

AN ORIGINAL English pig of the Large variety, closely related to pigs from Lancashire and Lincolnshire – colouring was variable, but basically white – it was in fact the forerunner of the Large White. In 1858, the winning boar at Chester weighed in at 1,148 lbs. The Old Yorkshire was used almost exclusively for bacon.

'No man should be allowed to be President, who does not understand hogs.'

HARRY TRUMAN

M WISCOMBE

$\mathcal{S}$ADDLEBACK

PIGS WITH this type of saddle marking, rather than spots or patches, are traditionally known as 'sheeted' – it may be a trait inherited from a belted Italian breed, the Cinta Senese, introduced into this country from Siena. The British Saddleback is a relatively recent amalgamation of the Old Essex and the Wessex Saddleback. Saddlebacks are said to be particularly good mothers, producing numerous healthy litters.

The largest pig ever recorded was Big Bill, an American Poland China hog, who weighed in at a staggering 182 stones, and measured 9 feet from snout to tail.

*L*INCOLNSHIRE CURLYCOAT

THIS WAS a large, jowly pig, lop-eared and with an abundance of long curly hair which protected it from the cold winds of its native Lincolnshire. Its good round back end and very fat body were once prized but when the trend for leaner meat came along this proved its downfall, and it is now extinct.

The first pigs in North America may have been 13 hogs introduced by Hernando de Soto, when he landed in Tampa Bay in 1539.

M. WISCOMBE.

OXFORD SANDY & BLACK

A MEDIUM-SIZED pig with plenty of sandy hair and dark blotches, this breed is said to have been in existence for at least two centuries. There may have been a connection with the Axford, which was bred from red pigs imported from Barbados and our native white 'unimproved' variety. They are popular today for their excellent temperament and good breeding qualities.

Lord Brougham expressed the hope that he would see the day when every man in the United Kingdom would read Bacon. 'It would be much better to the purpose if his lordship would use his influence that every man in the kingdom could eat bacon,' said William Cobbett.

HE LARGE WHITE

EVOLVED FROM a mixture of the native pigs of north west Europe and imported Chinese animals, the Large White was really indistinguishable from the Yorkshire. It was originally allowed to have some pale bluish spots on it, although after 1909 this was frowned upon. The most noted breeder of Large, Small, and Middle Whites in the mid-nineteenth century was Joseph Tuley, a weaver from Yorkshire, whose pigs attracted much attention at the Royal Show in 1851. The Large White eventually became Britain's most popular pig and has been exported all over the world.

'The actual lines of a pig (I mean a really fat pig) are among the loveliest, and most luxuriant in nature.'

G. K. CHESTERTON

M.WISCOMBE.

ERKSHIRE

AROUND BERKSHIRE in the mid-eighteenth century the use of clover swards as summer keep contributed to the popularity of this pig, which thrived on grazing. Originally parti-coloured black with white or red, the Berkshire was 'improved' in the second half of the nineteenth century by Lord Barrington, and then looked much as it does today, mostly black with just a little white on it.

'The time has come,' the
    Walrus said,
'to talk of many things:
of shoes, and ships, and
    sealing-wax,
of cabbages and kings,
and why the sea is boiling
    hot —
and whether pigs have
    wings.'

EDWARD LEAR

M.WISCOMBE.

AMWORTH

'A CURIOSITY', said one judge in 1876, describing the Tamworth as having 'a snout well-nigh the length of other pigs' bodies.' It used to be thought that this lean-fleshed variety was directly descended from the wild boar, or the old English forest pig, but nowadays it is thought to be related to the Axford, which took its distinctive red-gold colouring from the imported red Barbadan pig.

A carrion crow sat on an oak
Watching a tailor shape his cloak.
Wife, cried he, bring me my bow,
That I may shoot yon carrion crow.

The tailor shot and missed his mark,
And shot his own sow through the
    heart.
Wife, bring brandy in a spoon,
For our poor old sow is in a swoon.

The old sow died, the bells did toll,
And the little pigs prayed for the
    old sow's soul.
Zooks! quoth the tailor, I care not a
    louse,
For we'll have black pudding,
    chitterlings and souse!

TRADITIONAL

ARGE HAMPSHIRE

THIS AMERICAN variety is also known as the Thin Rind Pig, the Belted Kentucky, and the Ring Middle Pig. It is probably descended from the Wessex Saddleback, or the similar Old English breed that came from Northumberland and the Border Counties. In 1798 a Large Hampshire was recorded as weighing in at 1,624 lbs.

'The sight of flitches upon the rack tends more to keep a man from poaching and stealing than whole volumes of penal statutes... They are great softeners of the temper and promoters of domestic harmony.'

JOHN BERESFORD

THE OLD ULSTER

THIS IRISH pig was another old fashioned looking, large white variety, with heavy jowls and a squashed face that denoted the addition of Chinese blood in the eighteenth century. Its long ears were suited to a grazing existence. It became extinct around the middle of the twentieth century.

'Every cottage has a pig or two. These graze in the forest, and in the fall eat acorns and beech-nuts and the seed of ash.'

WILLIAM COBBETT

M WISCOMBE

ARGE BLACK

LARGE BLACKS have been exported to many hot countries around the world, as their dark skin makes them less likely to suffer from sunburn. Mrs Beeton's cookery book of 1861 mentions the exceptional 'fineness and delicacy' of their skin, their 'kindlier nature and aptitude to fatten'. They are believed to have originated in the southwest of England, particularly around Cornwall and Essex.

'The phrase "going the whole hog" must have originated in Ohio, for there they use up the entire carcases of about three-quarters of a million pigs a year.'

P. L. SIMMONDS

DUROC

THIS AMERICAN breed is a splendid mixture of British, African, Spanish and Portuguese red pigs. By 1900, the Duroc Jersey, as it was then known, was the most popular breed of pig in Nebraska and Iowa, the heart of the American 'hoglands'. Today the Duroc is one of the most numerous pigs in the world.

'The Prince Consort has, with great judgement, of late encouraged the collection of chestnuts in Windsor Park, and by giving a small reward to old people and children for every bushel collected, has not only found an occupation for many of the unemployed poor, but, by providing a gratuitous food for their pig, encouraged a feeling of providence and economy.'

MRS BEETON, 1861

M WISCOMBE.

CHESTER WHITE

NORTH AMERICA had no native pigs, and the first to arrive were those taken by the early settlers. This breed was developed mainly from the Lincolnshire Curlycoat and from the Cumberland, so is of great interest as both these varieties are now extinct. Its long coat makes it very hardy, an excellent outdoor pig.

Little pink pigs and none of them lean
Patches like truffles on satin-pink skin
More or less aping a nice galantine
Dappled with sun
Busily scampering devil-may-come
Fat little backs have a shimmering air
Glossily quivering everywhere
Jelly, each one.

EDMOND RUSTBARD

M WISCOMBE.

OLD ENGLISH

THE ORIGINAL Old English pig, as it existed in the eighteenth century, was a large, slab-sided and slow to mature animal, coarsely bristled and with lop ears. Its descendant from the West Country, once known as the Cornish White, or Devon Lop, is one of the biggest breeds in the country as well as one of the oldest. Well suited to the hilly cider orchards of its homeland it is still prevalent around Tavistock in Devon.

'If a hog be more than a year old he is the better for it. Make him fat by all means. If he can walk two or three hundred yards at a time he is not well-fatted. Lean bacon is the most wasteful thing that a family can use.'

WILLIAM COBBETT

M.WISCOMBE

LARGE WELSH

CLOSELY RELATED to the Long White Lop and the Cumberland and Ulster varieties, this popular, hardy type of large white pig may have had some connection with the Landrace, from northern Europe. Though the Cumberland and Ulster are both now extinct the Welsh continues to thrive.

'And here I cannot help mentioning a very ridiculous show, of a learned pig, which of late days attracted much of the public notice, and at the polite end of the town. This pig, which indeed was a large unwieldy hog, being taught to pick up letters written upon pieces of cards, and to arrange them at command, gave great satisfaction to all who saw him, and filled his Tormentor's pocket with money.'

JOSEPH STRUTT, 1789

M WISCOMBE

BAKEWELL'S PIG

NAMED AFTER Robert Bakewell, who became famous for his experiments in pig breeding, this is one of the earliest recorded attempts to produce an 'improved' pig. Bakewell crossed the dark chestnut with a rusty red, then brought in a celebrated black boar, to sire a pig of mixed colouring. This pig may have been the source of the old-fashioned 'plum pudding' type once common in Leicestershire.

The Bakewell was described by John M. Wilson, as having 'its belly nearly touching the ground and its eyes and snout looking as if they were almost absorbed into the body.'

'The pig has about him a natural, pleasant, hail-fellow well-met air, devoid of servility or insolence, which endears him to the English sensibility.'

W. H. HUDSON, *naturalist*